EDGE
BOOKS

The Unexplained

STONEHENGE

by **Matt Doeden**
Consultant:
Curtis Runnels, PhD
Professor of Archaeology
Department of Archaeology, Boston University
Boston, Massachusetts

Capstone
press®
Mankato, Minnesota

Edge Books are published by Capstone Press,
151 Good Counsel Drive, P.O. Box 669, Mankato, Minnesota 56002.
www.capstonepress.com

Library of Congress Cataloging-in-Publication Data
Doeden, Matt.
    Stonehenge / by Matt Doeden.
    p. cm.—(Edge books. The unexplained)
    Summary: "Describes Stonehenge, how it was built, and the theories of
why it was built"—Provided by publisher.
    Includes bibliographical references and index.
    ISBN-13: 978-0-7368-6762-7 (hardcover)
    ISBN-10: 0-7368-6762-7 (hardcover)
    1. Stonehenge (England)—Juvenile literature. 2. Wiltshire (England)—Antiquities—
Juvenile literature. 3. Megalithic monuments—England—Wiltshire—Juvenile literature.
I. Title. II. Series.
DA142.D64 2007
936.23'19—dc22
                          2006024425

Editorial Credits
Aaron Sautter, editor; Juliette Peters, set designer; Patrick D. Dentinger,
    book designer; Deirdre Barton, photo researcher/photo editor

Photo Credits
Corbis/Angelo Hornak, 9; Gideon Mendel, 5; M. Dillon, 28; Richard T. Nowitz, cover, 22;
    Roger Ressmeyer, 14–15, 19; Stapleton Collection, 17; Tom Bean, 23
Fortean Picture Library/Janet & Colin Bord, 27; Paul Broadhurst, 16
Getty Images Inc./Hulton Archive, 26; Peter Macdiarmid, 29
Index Stock Imagery/Terry Why, 20
Mary Evans Picture Library, 7, 10, 12, 13, 25

1 2 3 4 5 6 12 11 10 09 08 07

Table of Contents

Chapter 1: An Ancient Monument ... 4

Chapter 2: The Origin of
Stonehenge 8

Chapter 3: Lost Secrets Revealed ... 18

Chapter 4: Looking for Answers ... 24

FEATURES

Stonehenge Replicas................. 23

Preserving Stonehenge............. 29

Glossary 30

Read More 31

Internet Sites 31

Index 32

Chapter 1
An Ancient Monument

For hundreds of years, researchers had tried to solve Stonehenge's mysteries. Through the years, the ancient structure had revealed little.

But this day would be different. On July 10, 1953, archaeologist Richard Atkinson made an amazing discovery. As the huge stones cast long shadows across the Salisbury Plain, something caught Atkinson's eye. Looking closer, he found carvings in the stone. One was of a dagger. The second was a group of four axes. These ancient carvings had gone unseen for hundreds of years. But in the right light, they were unmistakable. The discovery would eventually help solve some of Stonehenge's many mysteries—who built it, and why?

Learn about:
• Ancient carvings
• The Druids
• Merlin

4

Stonehenge's long shadows creep across
the Salisbury Plain in southern England.

About Stonehenge

Stonehenge is one of the most famous and mysterious structures in the world. The large circle of stones has been standing for more than 4,000 years. What is it? Is it a temple? Is it an ancient device that tracks the planets? Or is it an enormous calendar? People have argued about these questions for hundreds of years.

Historians in the Middle Ages had few explanations for Stonehenge. Long ago, priests called Druids worshipped in the forest or open country. Some historians believed the Druids built Stonehenge as a church. But there is no evidence the Druids built Stonehenge or ever worshipped there.

Other people turned to legends for an explanation. One story says the wizard Merlin thought giants had built Stonehenge in Ireland. Merlin used powerful spells to move the stone blocks to England. He then rebuilt Stonehenge to honor a group of knights who had been killed in battle.

People have only recently begun to learn more about Stonehenge's real purpose and who built it. Many believe it was first built as a temple. But others believe it was used for far more.

People once thought the ancient Druids built Stonehenge. The Druids worshipped many gods and celebrated the change of seasons.

Chapter 2

The Origin of Stonehenge

We may never know all the details of who built Stonehenge or why. But through careful study, archaeologists can make a close guess about how Stonehenge was built.

Stonehenge was built over a long period of time. In about 3000 BC, Stonehenge began as little more than a large round ditch, a circle of holes, and a few stones. Nobody knows what purpose the holes and stones may have served.

Learn about:
• Parts of Stonehenge
• Building Stonehenge
• The Heel Stone

The large round ditch surrounding Stonehenge is easily seen from the air.

Heavy Lifting

The first step in building Stonehenge was lifting the large sarsen stones to an upright position. The builders used deer antlers to dig deep holes in the ground. Then they used ropes, levers, and the strength of many men to pull the stones into the big holes.

⬆ The sarsen stones were extremely heavy. It probably took hundreds of people to lift them into place.

Smaller stones, called lintels, were placed on top of the sarsens. The lintels helped form a complete, enclosed circle. Though smaller, the lintels were still heavy. Placing them atop the sarsens must have been difficult. Some people think the builders pulled the lintels up giant dirt ramps. Others think they used a system of strong stone or wooden platforms to lift the lintels little by little.

The largest and tallest stones, called trilithons, were placed at the center of the monument. Each included two huge upright stones, topped by one lintel. Five trilithons formed the shape of a horseshoe. A smaller horseshoe of bluestones stood inside the trilithon group. One last large stone, called the Altar Stone, was placed in the middle of the bluestone horseshoe.

The trilithons stand by themselves at the center of Stonehenge.

The Heel Stone was once called the Friar's Heel. Legends say the Devil threw the stone at a friar and struck him in the heel. The stone stuck in the ground, where it still stands today.

The Heel Stone stands on the outer edge of the Stonehenge site.

Whatever methods were used, building Stonehenge must have been backbreaking work. It took careful planning, many resources, and great patience to complete the job. But the result is a structure that has stood the test of time.

The ancient builders might have used Stonehenge for large ceremonies and festivals when it was complete.

Chapter 3

Lost Secrets Revealed

Scientists believe Stonehenge was sacred to ancient people for about 1,500 years. But over time, both the builders and Stonehenge's purpose were forgotten. The stones became a mystery. Some people began thinking the monument held ancient secrets. They imagined that the builders performed magic at Stonehenge. But no evidence has been found of any magical activities. By studying the stones closely, researchers have begun to understand some of Stonehenge's possible uses.

Learn about:
- The solstices
- Ancient burial mounds
- Carhenge

People once thought Stonehenge was used
for many kinds of mysterious activities.

Some scientists think Stonehenge may have been used to keep track of the moon and predict eclipses.

Astronomical Calendar

One of Stonehenge's purposes seems clear. The ancient stones work well as a calendar. A few stones mark the spots of the summer and winter solstices. These are the longest and shortest days of the year. At the summer solstice, the sun rises directly over the Heel Stone when viewed from within the stone circle. On the winter solstice, the sun sets between the two large stones of the center trilithon.

Scientists have also wondered if Stonehenge marked more than just the movements of the sun. In 1963, astronomer Gerald Hawkins used a computer to show how Stonehenge may have been used to predict eclipses. Scientists still debate his ideas today. But it seems that Stonehenge's builders must have known something about astronomy.

A Temple?

Most scientists believe Stonehenge was more than just a calendar. Several ancient burial mounds surround the area. These mounds hold valuable items such as gold and jewelry. It appears that rich and powerful people were buried near Stonehenge. Stonehenge may have had a religious meaning for the people buried there.

▲ These artifacts found at Stonehenge show the types of tools ancient people once used.

Stonehenge Replicas

Stonehenge has inspired several replicas around the world. In New Zealand, the Stonehenge Aotearoa shows how ancient people might have tracked the movements of the sun. Some replicas are less serious. In Nebraska, an artist built a replica of Stonehenge out of old cars. It's called Carhenge.

Chapter 4
Looking for Answers

For thousands of years, people have been fascinated with Stonehenge. Scientists have made progress in guessing Stonehenge's purposes. But who built it? Through the centuries, credit has gone to many groups.

Studying Stonehenge

In the mid-1600s, John Aubrey did one of the first full studies of Stonehenge. He carefully mapped out the monument and compared it to other stone circles in the area. Aubrey thought the Druids had built other stone circles in England. He guessed that the Druids likely built Stonehenge as well.

Learn about:
- John Aubrey and the Druids
- The Greeks and Romans
- Preservation efforts

Scientists have tried to solve Stonehenge's mysteries for hundreds of years.

For a long time after Aubrey's study, people thought the Druids had built Stonehenge. But later, some suggested the Romans built it when they ruled England. Then in 1953, Atkinson's discovery of carvings in the stones led many to believe the ancient Greeks were involved. The dagger carved into the stone looked a lot like a Greek dagger.

John Aubrey discovered 56 holes in the ground that follow Stonehenge's circular ditch. They're called the Aubrey holes.

In the 1960s, tests called radiocarbon dating suggested the building of Stonehenge began almost 5,000 years ago. This date ruled out Greek influence, since the ancient Greeks lived about 2,500 years ago. The Romans and Druids weren't in England at that time either. One mystery seems to be solved. Ancient people native to the area must have built Stonehenge.

▼ Some of the carvings Atkinson discovered have been darkened so they are easier to see.

Whatever its original purpose or who built it, Stonehenge remains an amazing and mysterious structure. The strange grouping of stones sparks people's imaginations. Though researchers have learned a lot, we'll probably never know the full story. The mystery of Stonehenge will capture our imaginations for a long time to come.

▲ Stonehenge's mysteries may never be completely understood.

Preserving Stonehenge

For centuries, people have walked among Stonehenge's mysterious stones. Many have had little respect for the site. Nearby farmers have taken parts of the stones for their buildings. Tourists have taken pieces of Stonehenge as souvenirs. Others have even painted graffiti on the old stones.

But since 1978, England's government has limited the number of visitors to Stonehenge. The government also plans to build a tunnel along one of the nearby roads. They hope the tunnel will reduce the effects of traffic on the site.

Stonehenge has stood for more than 4,000 years. Through preservation efforts, the ancient stones and their mysteries may stand for 4,000 more.

Glossary

archaeologist (ar-kee-OL-uh-jist)—a person who studies old buildings and objects to learn about the past

bluestone (BLOO-stone)—a type of stone made when volcanic lava cools; the smaller stones of Stonehenge are bluestones.

eclipse (i-KLIPS)—an astronomical event in which the earth's shadow passes over the moon or the moon's shadow passes over the earth

friar (FRY-ur)—a religious man who has promised to devote his life to God

lintel (LINT-el)—a horizontal sarsen stone that rests across the top of two larger upright stones

radiocarbon dating (ray-dee-oh-KAR-buhn DAYT-ing)—a method of measuring the type of carbon in an object to determine how old it is

sarsen (SAR-suhn)—a type of sandstone; the largest stones of Stonehenge are sarsens.

solstice (SOL-stiss)—the days of the year when the sun rises at its northernmost and southernmost points

trilithon (tri-LITH-thon)—a grouping of two upright sarsens supporting a horizontal lintel

Read More

Lynette, Rachel. *Stonehenge*. Great Structures in History. Detroit: KidHaven Press, 2005.

Malone, Caroline, and Nancy Stone Bernard. *Stonehenge*. Digging for the Past. New York: Oxford University Press, 2002.

Petrini, Catherine M. *Stonehenge*. Wonders of the World. Farmington Hills, Mich.: KidHaven Press, 2006.

Internet Sites

FactHound offers a safe, fun way to find Internet sites related to this book. All of the sites on FactHound have been researched by our staff.

Here's how:
1. Visit *www.facthound.com*
2. Choose your grade level.
3. Type in this book ID **0736867627** for age-appropriate sites. You may also browse subjects by clicking on letters, or by clicking on pictures and words.
4. Click on the **Fetch It** button.

FactHound will fetch the best sites for you!

Index

Altar Stone, 14
archaeologists. See scientists
Atkinson, Richard, 4, 26, 27
Aubrey, John, 24, 26

bluestones, 11, 14
builders, 11, 12, 13, 17, 18,
    21, 27
building Stonehenge, 8, 11–16
burial mounds, 22

Carhenge, 23
carvings, 4, 26, 27

Druids, 6, 7, 21, 24, 26, 27

Greeks, 26, 27

Hawkins, Gerald, 21
Heel Stone, 16, 21

lintels, 13, 14

magic, 6, 18
Marlborough Downs, 11
Merlin, 6
moving stones, 10, 11
mysteries, 4, 6, 18, 19, 25,
    27, 28

Prescelli Mountains, 11
preservation, 29

radiocarbon dating, 27
Romans, 26, 27
round ditch, 8, 9

Salisbury, England, 4, 5
sarsen stones, 11, 12, 13
scientists, 4, 8, 11, 18, 20, 21,
    22, 24, 25, 28
South Wales, 11
Stonehenge Aotearoa, 23
summer solstice, 21

tools, 11, 12, 22
tourists, 29
trilithons, 14, 15, 21

uses for Stonehenge, 18, 19, 28
    astronomy, 20, 21
    calendar, 6, 21
    ceremonies, 17
    eclipses, 20, 21
    temple, 6

winter solstice, 21